Hide and Seek

Hide and Seek
Published by Passage Point Publishing, Denver, CO

Publisher's Cataloging-in-Publication data

Names: Lintonsmith, Susan, author. | Drew, Tristram, illustrator.
Title: Hide and seek / Susan Lintonsmith ; illustrated by Tristram Drew.
Description: Denver, CO: Passage Point Publishing, 2021. | Summary: Ten-year-old Spencer and his annoying little brother, Justin, have just moved to a new neighborhood. Spencer has no friends and a strange new nanny who he's convinced has secrets. He's grumpy ... until he and Justin discover the couch!
Identifiers: ISBN: 978-1-7368910-0-1 (paperback)
Subjects: LCSH Siblings--Juvenile fiction. | Moving, Household--Juvenile fiction. | Fantasy fiction. | CYAC Siblings--Fiction. | Moving, Household--Fiction. | BISAC JUVENILE FICTION / Fantasy & Magic | JUVENILE FICTION / Readers / Intermediate | JUVENILE FICTION / Family / Siblings
Classification: LCC PZ7.1.L5645 Hid| DDC [Fic]--dc23

ISBN: 978-1-7368910-0-1

Illustrations by Tristram Drew
Cover and Interior design by Laura Drew
Editing by Shelly Wilhelm

PASSAGE
POINT
PUBLISHING

UNDER THE COUCH

BOOK **1**

Hide and Seek

SUSAN LINTONSMITH

To my sons, Spencer and Justin, who encouraged me to write books based on the stories I told them when they were young.

CONTENTS

CHAPTER
1

Spencer eyed Lori suspiciously. Something wasn't right about her. He wasn't sure what it was, but he'd figure it out. She didn't fool him.

Lori sat at the kitchen table playing checkers with his seven-year-old brother, Justin. The two of them were laughing and in a good mood, but Spencer was not. It was the beginning of summer, and he should be back at his old house hanging with his friends at the pool. Instead, he was forty miles away, stuck inside with his annoying little brother and a strange new nanny. This was not the summer he wanted. He was mad at his mom for making him move so she could be closer to her new job. He was mad that they moved into a neighborhood with mostly empty lots. He hadn't seen any kids his age and wondered how he was supposed to make new friends. And now he had to start a new school for fifth grade in the fall. He didn't want to be the new kid. He was mad and grumpy . . . and hot!

"Justin, quit being so loud," he snapped. Spencer was ten years old and had little patience for his younger brother. Justin was cheering every time he took one of Lori's checkers. Spencer knew Lori was letting Justin win. He observed her closely. She had been their nanny for two weeks now, and he knew nothing about her. She started when they moved into their new house. He was hoping for a younger person, but his mother claimed she had trouble finding someone for the summer. Finally, through a friend of his grandmother's, she found Lori.

She was in her forties, like his parents. She was short and a little heavy, with short black hair. Spencer studied her strange glasses. The lenses were thick with big black frames that took up most of her face. He didn't understand why his family thought she was so great. His parents were happy that she arrived on time every morning and in a good mood. Justin thought she was nice and liked that she played with him. Spencer knew Lori liked Justin more than she liked him. She thought Justin was cute and funny, and she laughed at him a lot. Spencer didn't care. He didn't really like her either. He thought she was odd and knew she was hiding something. He planned to figure it out.

Spencer stopped staring at Lori and looked out the window above the sink. He watched the tractor on the empty lot next door dig into the ground and lift a pile of dirt, twist, and drop it to the side. The hole was bigger than it had been that morning, and the dirt pile was getting higher. He hoped a family with boys his age would buy the house.

Spencer jumped as Justin screamed again. He had won the game. Spencer turned and yelled at him to stop being so annoying.

Lori sighed. "Spencer, go do something."

"I'd like to play video games, but I can't, thanks to Justin!"

"No, Mom took video games away from you because you hit me." Justin lifted his sleeve to show Lori the bruise on his arm. Lori frowned at Spencer.

"No, you got in trouble first," Spencer said, trying to redeem himself to Lori. "Justin spilled red juice on the new carpet and then stupidly covered it with Mom's white pillow." He turned back to Justin, pointing his finger at him. "You're the one who put her in a bad mood, and you got video games taken away first."

Lori sighed heavily again. Spencer knew she was annoyed. She didn't like their fighting.

She glanced at the kitchen clock. Spencer looked up at it and saw that it was nearly time for her TV show to start. She got tired in the afternoons and liked to relax and watch her program. Spencer didn't like her show. It was just a bunch of adults talking about boring things. He usually would play video games while she watched TV. But now he couldn't play for a week because he had gotten in trouble for hitting Justin. His mom said he had to stop being so grumpy and stop picking on his brother. He thought, *I'm grumpy because she made us move and ruined my summer!*

Spencer watched as Lori got up from the table and started making her tea. She put water on the stove to boil, and then dug deep into her large brown shoulder bag and pulled out a strange-looking tea bag. Spencer eyed her shoulder bag. It was large, even bigger than his mom's new leather briefcase that his dad had gotten for her when she landed her new job.

"Is that real leather?" Spencer asked. It looked to him like it was made from suede and leather. Lori looked at him like he had three heads.

"Of course not! It's faux," she told him. "I love animals. I would never wear or have something made from them." Spencer didn't know what *faux* was but understood that it wasn't from animals. He sighed and turned to look back out the window. He knew she was tired from their long morning at the park. She took them to the park every morning. She enjoyed walking through the wooded area and sitting on the grass while they played. Spencer knew she loved nature, and now he knew that she loved animals too.

"Justin, why don't you do your reading now and then I'll play something with you when my show is over," Lori suggested.

"Nooo, I don't want to read," Justin whined.

Spencer knew his brother hated to read and snickered, "He doesn't know how to read. He can't even read a picture book!" Justin got up from the table to lunge at Spencer, but Lori stepped in the way to stop him.

She turned angrily toward Spencer. "You know you're not supposed to tease him about his reading." Spencer knew it, but he didn't care. He loved that it made his brother mad.

No one could understand why Justin struggled with reading. Spencer had overheard his parents talking about it. His mother was concerned that he'd be behind when he started second grade, so she decided that he needed more practice. She was making both boys read every day during the summer. Spencer didn't mind as long as he could read books about space. He loved reading about the planets and their moons in the solar system. He was currently reading a book about the Earth's moon. He had checked out other books on the planets and stars from the library to read next. He wanted to travel in space when he got older. His dad joked with him that his mind was already in space. It was okay for his dad to tease him, but he hated when Justin did it. Sometimes he just got lost in his thoughts and tuned out what was happening around him. He didn't see anything wrong with that.

He watched Lori stir her tea as she walked into the family room. Justin followed behind her, whining that he didn't want to read.

"Okay, I'll read with you when my show is over," Lori said as she climbed into the big chair with the footstool. She always gave in to Justin. She turned to Spencer. "Play with your brother. And be nice to him." Spencer noticed that she wasn't asking. Spencer locked eyes with her. Her dark brown eyes looked bigger through her thick glasses. She looked serious, and he decided not to argue.

CHAPTER
2

"What do you want to do, since it's your fault we can't play video games?" Spencer asked, thinking that the last thing he wanted to do right now was play with his brother.

"Let's play hide-and-seek," Justin suggested, his big blue eyes lighting up.

Spencer shook his head. "No, I'm not in the mood for playing silly games." He knew his brother loved playing hide-and-seek, especially in the new house.

"Please? I didn't tell Mom that you pushed me down yesterday when she asked what happened to my knees."

Spencer thought about that. Justin could have gotten him in more trouble than he was already in. His parents were unhappy with his bad moods and for picking on his brother. Finally, he gave in. What else were they going to do?

"Okay, but no changing hiding places, and the basement is off-limits." The basement was unfinished and full of moving boxes. He didn't want to look too hard.

Justin smiled and agreed. "I'll hide first. Count slowly," he said as he ran out of the kitchen.

Spencer walked over and leaned against the kitchen sink. He didn't close his eyes or start counting. Instead, he looked out the window and watched the tractor's claw bring up another huge pile of dirt. He tried to listen for Justin's footsteps but couldn't hear anything over the tractor next door and the TV in the family room. He hoped that Justin didn't go upstairs.

After watching the tractor for a few minutes, Spencer turned and yelled, "Here I come!" He saw Lori jump in her chair, which almost made him laugh.

He looked around. He knew Justin wasn't in the kitchen. He walked toward Lori, but she looked over and shook her head to tell him Justin wasn't in the family room. He looked in the game room where their video games were locked away in a cabinet for the week. The game room was really an office that his parents were letting the boys use for playing video games and for storing their games and Justin's toys until the basement was finished. He went into the living room and looked around. There was no place to hide in the living room except under the large couch. He got down on the floor and lifted the couch skirt. He took a quick peek under, but it was dark, and he didn't see anything.

He continued searching the rest of the main floor, with no luck.

Spencer groaned. Justin must have gone upstairs. Spencer climbed the stairs to search the second floor. He looked through both of their bedrooms. They each had their own room and shared a bathroom. He looked through the guest room, which was next to his room. His parents' room was on the other end of the hall, but they weren't supposed to play in there. He couldn't find Justin, so he decided to look through his parents' room anyway. Justin wasn't in there. Spencer sighed heavily. He was not having fun. He couldn't find him on either floor, and they had agreed that the basement was off-limits.

Spencer grumbled as he went back down the stairs and returned to the living room. He stared at the oversized cream-colored couch. Justin liked to hide under it because it was tall and had a skirt that touched the floor. Their dad had bought it a few weeks ago at a store that sold antiques. It didn't look old since the fabric was almost new.

Spencer got down on his hands and knees and lifted the couch skirt again. He wondered if he hadn't looked well enough the first time. "I got you," he called, even though he couldn't see him. "Justin?" There was no response. It was unusual for Justin to stay quiet. Spencer made farting noises with his mouth. That usually made Justin laugh. Still no response. Spencer cursed under his breath. Justin was usually easy to find.

Frustrated, Spencer started to pull his head back from under the couch but stopped. He thought he heard something. The tractor next door was shut off, so the noise wasn't coming from outside. He put his right ear against the wood floor and plugged his left ear with his finger, listening intently. He heard the noise again. It was very faint, but he could make out his name. It had to be Justin calling him, but he sounded far away. *Is he in the basement?*

"I said the basement was off-limits!" Now he was really mad. Spencer ran down the

13

basement stairs and turned on the lights. He saw boxes and containers covering the cement floor. "I said no basement!" He looked around but didn't see movement. "Come out — game over!" He crossed his arms and waited for Justin to appear. "I'm not playing anymore. I'm going to my room." Justin was always goofing around, and Spencer was NOT in the mood for it. He waited for Justin to come out, but his brother didn't appear. Angrily, Spencer quickly looked around the basement but didn't find him. He could have sworn he heard Justin's voice when he was under the couch, but he wasn't in the basement. *Where is he?*

Spencer left the basement and was starting to head upstairs to his room when he stopped. It was strange that he couldn't find Justin. Or that Justin hadn't come out of his hiding place by now. Spencer knew that Justin wasn't very patient. It wasn't like him to stay hidden this long. Spencer wondered if something could have happened.

He looked behind him toward the living room. Finally, he went back to the couch, where he had last heard him. He got down on the floor and lifted the couch skirt again. "This isn't funny!" Spencer stuck his head under and pressed his ear against the floor like he had done the last time. The tractor next door had started back up, so this time he couldn't hear Justin's voice.

Spencer was starting to worry. He could feel the sweat pooling on his forehead. He wondered if he should get Lori. He didn't feel like looking anymore, and he didn't want to go under the couch. It was dark and dusty under there — a perfect place for spiders. Two things he hated were the dark and spiders. He decided to let Lori deal with it.

He went into the family room and called her name. She didn't answer. He looked in her chair, but she wasn't there. He glanced around but didn't see her. *First Justin disappears and then Lori?* He didn't have time to deal with finding Lori. He knew something was wrong.

He could feel it in his gut. He had to find Justin, without Lori's help. Besides, he figured Lori would just blame *him* for losing his brother.

Spencer jogged back to the living room. He knew he had heard Justin's voice under the couch. He didn't imagine that. He dropped down to the floor and lifted the skirt. He took a deep breath and crawled under. He pushed his entire body to the wall, where he initially thought Justin was hiding. He reached around to see if Justin was there, but only felt a little dust. He still couldn't hear anything but the tractor next door. He was about to slide back out when suddenly, he felt like he was falling off a ledge!

CHAPTER 3

How can I be falling? His stomach leapt into his chest, and he yelled out. He swung his arms around, reaching for something to grab onto. Then, he felt a cool, slick surface under him. *Am I on a slide?* He tried to turn around and ended up on his stomach, heading face-first down the steep slope. He kept his arms in front of him to protect his face as he went around turns. He could feel the high curved sides holding him on the slide as he slid down and around in tighter circles. He was going so fast. He tried to drag his feet to slow down, but that was useless; the surface was too slick.

What is happening? It reminded him of the long winding slide at the water park. But there was no water and no park. After countless turns, he felt himself fly off the slide. He landed on the ground with a *thud*, flat on his stomach. He got the wind knocked out of him. He gasped for air as he lifted his head. He could smell the rubber from the mat under him. He took a deep breath . . . as something grabbed him!

Spencer screamed as he swung wildly, trying to break free from the hand that was grasping his arm.

"Ouch! Stop hitting!" a voice cried.

He stopped swinging. "Justin! What the heck?" He was so shocked he didn't know what to say.

"You found me!" Justin said as he bounced on top of Spencer. "I kept yelling for you, and you found me!"

Spencer was dazed. He felt like he was waking up from a strange dream. He pushed Justin off of him and sat up, holding his queasy stomach. He looked around. It was fairly dark, and he couldn't make out where he was. He blinked his eyes several times and wished he had a flashlight.

"What just happened? How did we fall *under* the couch?" Spencer couldn't mask his trembling voice.

"I don't know," Justin replied, shaking his head.

"I don't understand. Where the heck are we? I just don't understand how this happened."

"I don't know. I was hiding under the couch, and I heard you say that you were coming. I pushed closer to the wall so you couldn't see me. Next thing I knew, I fell onto that slide and landed here." Justin pointed to the slide and then the padded floor.

Spencer's eyes were adjusting to the darkness. He could see that they were in a hallway. He felt chills on his arms and legs. It was cold and damp in this place. "I looked everywhere for you. I thought you were goofing around." Spencer remembered being really mad at him.

"I wasn't," Justin said. "And I yelled for you as loud as I could."

Spencer could hear that Justin's voice was hoarse from yelling. "I know, I heard you. That's why I ended up here." Spencer looked at Justin, whose dark blond hair was messy and hanging into his eyes. He expected Justin to be frightened, but he seemed excited. He was actually smiling. "I can't imagine being alone down here," Spencer said softly, more to himself. He was still trying to understand where they were. The thought of being lost somewhere under their couch made Spencer's stomach hurt more. He slowly stood up and turned to look at the slide.

"Cool slide, huh?" Justin asked, grinning.

"That was a fun ride!"

"Until the landing," Spencer said, still holding his stomach. He looked around and shook his head, confused. "I'm just trying to understand all of this. Anyone else down here?"

Justin shook his head. "Nope."

"Did you see any stairs or elevator . . . or any way to get back up?"

"No, it's just a long hallway with a ginormous door at the end." Justin pointed away from the slide and into the darkness. "But I couldn't get it open."

Spencer walked over to the slide and ran his hand across the smooth surface. It was shiny and looked like stainless steel. It was wide and curved in a "U" shape. He had never seen a slide like this before.

"Then we need to go back *up* the slide." Spencer pointed as he leaned his head back to look up. He could only see a small part of the slide before it disappeared in the darkness.

"I tried climbing it a *bazillion* times. I couldn't get past that second turn." Justin was looking up the slide with Spencer. Justin was athletic, so Spencer was surprised to hear his brother couldn't get far up the slide. He knew it was long and steep but figured he was stronger than Justin, so he would have a better chance of making it back up. He had to. They had to get back to their house.

Spencer stepped onto the slide and started climbing. He got to the first turn and slid back down. He turned around and tried again. This time, he got nearly to the second turn before slipping down to the bottom. He saw what Justin was talking about. It seemed to be even slicker near the second curve. He was wearing his good sneakers but couldn't get traction on the surface. He tried several more times. He tried holding the side of the slide to pull himself up. It was awkward and slow as he pulled himself along. He got to the second turn and slid back down to the bottom again.

After trying for a while, he stopped. "I need to rest. And think." He was trying not to panic. *What is this place?* He walked around the slide but couldn't see anything behind it. He only saw darkness and a wall. The slide fed into a long hallway, like Justin had said. At the bottom of the slide was a rubber mat, which had helped to break his fall. The flooring in the hall was like rubber gym mats.

He looked up at the high ceiling. He figured it had to be over fifteen feet high since he was nearly five feet tall. The walls were different than anything he had ever seen. They were shiny, unlike the painted plaster walls in their house. He couldn't tell if they were mirrored or a shiny steel like the slide. As he stared at the wall, he could almost make out his reflection. He could see his light brown hair and green shirt. He froze. He thought he saw movement in the wall, next to his reflection. The hair on the back of his neck stood up. He looked around to see if he had seen Justin's reflection, but his brother was down the hallway.

Spencer's throat was dry and his legs felt weak as he looked around for a light switch. He didn't like the dark. He looked on both sides of the hallway but didn't see any light switches. The only light he could see seemed to be coming from *inside* the walls. He stepped closer to the wall and peered in. Then something grabbed him.

CHAPTER
4

Spencer jumped and tried to break free from the grasp.

"Geez, you need to relax!" Justin said as he backed away.

"You need to stop grabbing me!" Spencer felt jumpy in this creepy place, and Justin wasn't helping. "What do you want?"

"I need your help opening the door," Justin said. "It's too heavy for me."

"No!" Spencer said. He did not like the idea of going down a dark hallway. "Great place for huge spiders," he mumbled. He knew Justin hated spiders nearly as much as he did. Both of them had complained to their parents about how many spiders were in the fields around their new house.

"I didn't see any. Come on," Justin said, skipping down the hallway, not waiting for him. "Come help me."

Spencer sighed. He was worried about getting home and thought maybe the door could be the way back. He didn't see any other options. He hoped the door led to a staircase. Or better yet, an elevator. Spencer looked back and forth at the walls as he walked down the hall. He wondered if his mind was playing tricks on him. It seemed as if something in the wall was walking with him. He shook his head to clear it. It had to be his own reflection.

"Isn't this door huge?" Justin asked

when Spencer got to the end of the hallway. Spencer nodded. He eyed the black metal door. It had to be over twelve feet tall and eight feet wide. The door handle was a metal latch. Both looked big and heavy. He looked around but didn't see any signs for an exit, stairs, or an elevator.

"I don't think this door leads back to our house. Let's keep trying the slide," Spencer said as he started to head back down the hall. "There's got to be a way up the slide. We just have to figure it out."

"I think we should try going through this door," Justin said. Spencer turned and saw that Justin had his little hands on the big handle and was using his weight to try and open it.

"No, don't open it!" Spencer ran back.

Justin continued pulling. "I want to see what's on the other side."

Spencer reached out and grabbed the handle to stop him. Both of their hands were on the handle at the same time when the giant door slowly swung toward them. It opened

27

about two feet and stopped. Shocked, Spencer jumped back. He could see what looked like moonlight spilling through the door into the dark hallway. *Does the door lead outside?*

"Don't go through it!" Spencer ordered. But it was too late. Justin had already slipped through the opening.

"Wow! This place is cool!" Justin said.

Spencer stepped into the opening and pressed his body against the door, sticking his foot against the base. He wasn't going to let the heavy door close. "Get back here!" he yelled to Justin, who was running around the big room. It looked like the room was a giant circle. Justin was yelling about all the doors in the room. Spencer continued ordering him to come back. Finally, Justin returned to the hallway door. His face was flushed with excitement, and he pushed his messy hair out of his blue eyes.

"You need to see this room!"

Angrily, Spencer reached out and grabbed his brother's blue shirt and pulled him to the door. "Stand right here and don't let it shut," he instructed as he moved his foot to let Justin stand in the space.

"But I want to see the rest of the room," Justin protested.

"No! Stay right here. I'm going to see if I can find an elevator or stairs. Don't let that door shut, or we may not be able to get back." His words scared him more than they scared Justin. He didn't know what they would do if they couldn't get back into the hallway.

Spencer walked inside the room and called back, "I'll look quickly and then we'll get back to the slide." He sighed. He didn't know how they were going to get up the steep and slick slide. He had to find a way back. He looked around for an exit sign. He could see better in this room than he could in the hallway. The room was lighter and warmer. And it smelled nice — like an evening breeze. It felt like he was outside.

"Whoa," he said under his breath as he took in the huge circular room. The walls were covered with doors of all different shapes, sizes, and colors. He started to slowly circle the room, studying all the incredible doors. Every door was unique. There were doors in nearly every size, from gigantic to quite small. He saw many different shapes as well. His eyes were drawn to the shiny and bright-colored doors. He looked up and down the walls as he walked. "They're like snowflakes," he said. He had learned that no two snowflakes were alike.

He only meant to look for stairs or an elevator and then get back to the hallway door, but he found himself lost in the amazement of this peculiar room. The walls were over two stories tall. He bent his head back to view the ceiling. It was amazing! It reminded him of the ceiling at the planetarium that his third-grade class had visited on a field trip. The huge dome-shaped ceiling looked like a night sky. There were so many bright shiny stars and moons. *Moons?* He tilted his head back further. He counted *four* full moons! They were all perfectly shaped circles.

He furrowed his brow. *Why four?* He couldn't think of a planet with exactly four moons in the solar system. He went through the planets in order. Mercury and Venus didn't have moons. Earth had one and Mars had two. He was fairly sure Jupiter and Saturn each had more than sixty moons. He knew Uranus had twenty-seven known moons and Neptune had fourteen. He was confused which planet this ceiling was trying to replicate. He then studied the stars to see if he could find the big or little dipper. He frowned. He didn't recognize any of the star formations.

"Isn't this place cool?"

Spencer jerked his head back and spun around to see Justin behind him. He was so lost in the ceiling that he had forgotten about his brother. Panicked, he looked over at the giant black door that Justin was supposed to be holding. "The door!"

Justin turned to look. The black door was closed.

CHAPTER 5

"Are you kidding me? I told you to hold the door open!" Spencer shouted as he ran back to the door.

Justin followed behind him. "But you were taking a long time."

Spencer got to the door and tried to open it. The big handle wouldn't move. *Is it locked?* He tried pushing it, using all his weight, but it didn't budge. He was sweating, and he could feel his heart beating fast. "What have you done?" He turned and glared at his brother. His face felt hot. "I told you to hold it open!"

Justin blinked innocently. "I didn't know it would lock."

"Now we're stuck in here, and I have no idea how we're going to get back!" Spencer said, looking frantically around for a button or anything that could open the door. He couldn't find anything. He kept trying to open the door, with no luck. "Now what do we do?"

"Let's try one of the other doors," Justin said. "There's a ton of them." Justin ran over to the wall and started trying to open the doors.

"Don't touch anything! You've already caused enough trouble."

"But maybe one of these will take us back to our house," Justin suggested.

"Or they could take us further away. We could get really lost . . . forever." Spencer couldn't understand why Justin didn't think of these things. He just acted and didn't think about the costs. "Look, at least we know this big one leads us back to the slide." Spencer motioned to the big metal door.

Justin wasn't listening. He was busy trying every door. Spencer was angry but also amazed that his brother wasn't freaked out like he was. Justin looked like he was having fun. Spencer watched him try several more doors. They all seemed to be locked. Spencer looked around the room, wondering if there were keys or another way to open the doors. His eyes were drawn to a round glowing structure in the middle of the room. *How did I not see that before?* he wondered. As he looked at it, the glow seemed to get brighter.

"I don't see handles on some of these doors," Justin said as he continued around the room. "How are you supposed to open doors if there are no handles?"

Spencer didn't answer. He was focused on the glowing object and only half-listening. He walked slowly to the middle of the room.

Justin said, "Maybe you use a magical phrase or something."

At that comment, Spencer stopped and turned. "What? Are you kidding me?"

"No, you know, like Ali Baba says *open sesame*? That opened a door."

"To a cave," Spencer replied.

"Yah! And there was a bunch of treasure on the other side. Do you think we'll find treasure behind one of these doors?"

Spencer glared at him. "No."

"Then why are all these doors here?" Justin started jumping around, waving his arms, and shouting different phrases. "Open sesame! Open says me! Open sesame seed bun! Open this door or I'll blow the house down!" He kept at it for a while, making up phrases and shouting at the doors. It wasn't working, but he seemed to be enjoying himself. The sillier his commands were, the harder he laughed at himself. He ignored Spencer's shouts to stop.

Spencer wasn't amused and didn't understand how Justin could be having fun

at a time like this. Irritated, he turned back to the round structure in the center of the room. It started glowing even brighter. He was awed by the beautiful blue glow. As he stepped closer, he saw that it was a giant marble. It was perfectly round and nearly a foot taller than him. It was enchanting with its milky white swirls that looked like clouds against a deep blue sky. Spencer leaned against the structure and peered in. He felt like he could see *into* it. His mind started to relax, and he felt a little lightheaded. The deep blue started to sway with him. He pulled away, uncomfortable with the feeling.

He continued looking at the marble. Then, from the corner of his eye, he saw the white milky forms start to move toward him. He backed up several more feet and rubbed his eyes. Then he looked back at the marble. This time, he didn't see any movement.

"This whole situation is making me crazy!" Spencer yelled. Justin was still running around shouting commands at the doors. "And that's not helping!" Spencer added. He felt grumpier now than he had felt earlier in the day. This was all Justin's fault. *Why do I have such an annoying little brother?*

Spencer turned back to the marble. He wanted to climb on top of the structure. He thought he could get a better view of the circular room. He struggled to climb the smooth surface. He ran several times and tried jumping up on it. Finally, he jumped high onto the marble and pulled himself up.

Once on top, he sat down and looked into the marble. His mind stopped racing, and he felt his body relax again. As he gazed into the beautiful blue, he felt like he was floating around with the white swirls. Then the swirls moved away, and through the blue he could see a small box on the ground. As he got closer, he saw that the box was actually a house. Inside the house, he could see an image of a boy his age sitting on a couch. Spencer suddenly felt a heavy pain in his heart. He could feel the boy's great sadness. Spencer tried to ask the boy what was wrong. The pain was overwhelming. He knew this boy was lonely. Then he understood that the boy didn't have any friends. He had no one to play with. He desperately wanted a brother. Spencer tried to understand. *Does the boy not have a brother . . . or had something happened to him?* The boy lifted his head and looked up at Spencer. It was as if the boy knew Spencer was watching him. Spencer could see his sad blue eyes. He knew those eyes! He nearly fell off the marble when he saw that the boy looked exactly like him!

CHAPTER
6

"That's so cool," he heard a voice say.

Spencer jerked his head up. His head felt groggy, and he was sweating. He rubbed his temples and tried to clear his head. He could still feel the pain in his heart.

"Looks like a giant marble," Justin said. Spencer looked down and for the second time that day, he was happy to see Justin.

Justin reached out his hand for Spencer to grab. "Pull me up."

Spencer pushed his hand away. "No, not enough room."

Justin shrugged and returned to looking at the blue structure. "These white things look like clouds." He stopped circling the marble and bent down. "Looks like they make a word over here."

"What are you talking about?" Spencer, now more alert, glanced down toward Justin. "What's the word?"

"To . . . get . . . her. Who's her? Who are they talking about?" Justin scrunched up his nose, staring at the word.

"What? That doesn't make sense." Spencer slid down the giant marble and looked at the word. He read it out loud. "TOGETHER! Not TO . . . GET . . . HER! You're a terrible reader!"

"I was just sounding it out. It's hard to read cloud writing." Justin continued to look at the word. "What do you think it means?"

"Seriously?" Spencer groaned. "It's like,

42

you don't do it by yourself, you do it with someone else . . . "

"I know what *together* means. I'm not stupid! I meant, what's the message? It's a clue, right?"

Spencer thought about that. *Could it be a clue to getting out of this place?* "Maybe," he said.

"I wonder what we're supposed to do together," Justin said, his eyes big and his face flushed with excitement. "You should try some of these commands with me!"

Spencer didn't understand how his brother found this fun. He didn't want to shout commands at the doors. That was crazy. But he couldn't think of a better idea. He would try anything to get out of there and back home. "Okay."

"Okay?" Justin sounded surprised. "Let's start with this one!" He pointed to one of the biggest doors in the room.

"No! Let's start with the one that gets us back to the hallway. We have to get back to the slide."

Justin looked around at all the doors in the room and reluctantly followed Spencer. They stood in front of the black metal door and shouted different phrases together. Spencer felt like an idiot but knew Justin was having a great time. No matter what they shouted, the door didn't budge. Spencer tried the handle again. It didn't move.

"It's not working. Nothing is working. We're stuck!" Spencer yelled.

"Come on, let's try one of these other doors," Justin said. Spencer watched him skip back into the circular room. "Come on!" Justin called from the other side of the room.

Spencer grudgingly walked toward his brother. "Look, we can try a few doors, but no big or scary ones. Only normal doors."

"That's boring," Justin mumbled.

After arguing over several doors, they finally agreed on a square door made out of dark wood. Spencer thought it might be about six feet tall since it was more than a foot taller than him. He had never seen a square door before. "Interesting doorknob," he said. It looked like a small cube.

"Square like the door," Justin noted. "Let's try to open it . . . *to get her.*"

Spencer half-smiled. He was feeling anxious and wanted to get home. They tried several different ways to open the door, but nothing worked. They stopped and stared at the door for several minutes. Then Spencer had a thought.

"You know, the hallway door opened when we had our hands on the handle at the same time. Let's try that."

Spencer placed his left hand on the square knob. Justin nodded and put his left hand next to Spencer's.

"Okay, turn it to the right." They turned it together, and the door immediately opened.

"We did it!" Justin exclaimed as he started through the door. Spencer held his arm out to block him.

"Stop. Let me go first to see if there's any danger. You stand here and hold the door open. And this time, don't let it close!"

Spencer walked into a square room that looked like a huge playground filled with different sized cubes. The blocks were made from various types of materials. "A square door with a square knob leading into a square room filled with square blocks," Spencer said out loud. He looked at the walls around the room. There were different sized square pieces made from several types of materials hanging on the walls. In the center of the room was a square table with two little square stumps for chairs.

Spencer walked around the room, looking for an exit or any way to get back to the house. After searching the room, he walked over to the square table and sat down on one of the stumps to think.

"These are cute chairs," Justin said as he sat down on the other stump. Spencer jumped at his brother's voice. He swung around to look at the door.

"Are you kidding me? You let the door close . . . *again*?" Spencer yelled. He couldn't believe it had happened twice. He started to run toward the door and then stopped abruptly. He looked at the wall, stunned. "Where's the door?"

"Huh?" Justin turned around to look.

The door they had just come through was gone.

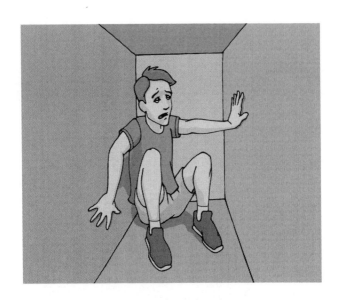

CHAPTER
7

Spencer ran over to where the door had been. He felt around. The wall was solid. There was no evidence that a door was ever there. He turned and looked accusingly at Justin. "What happened to the door?"

"It was right there. I left it standing open," Justin said, pointing to the wall. He spun around to look at the other walls in the room.

Spencer watched him. "You think the door *moved* to another wall?"

"Well, where did it go?" Justin asked as he looked at the wall where the door used to be. "You can't lose a door."

"Yet somehow you did," Spencer growled. "I can't believe this! I told you to hold it open. Twice, Justin! You let the doors close two times!"

"Maybe it's just playing hide-and-seek with us," Justin suggested.

"What?" Spencer shouted, getting madder by the minute. "A door can't move, and it certainly can't hide!" He was frustrated with his brother and the entire situation. "Now we're stuck in this strange square room because you didn't hold it open like I told you."

"I think it's hiding."

"Stop talking!" Spencer felt hot and his head was starting to pound. He didn't have the patience to listen to Justin's nonsense. He walked back to the stump and sat down. He put his head in his trembling hands. "We're stuck in a strange square room somewhere under our couch. We can't get back to the circular room, so we can't get back into the hallway to the slide . . . a slide that we can't climb. And there are no stairs or elevators. I don't understand *any* of this!" He knew he was ranting, but he was ready to explode. "I didn't want to play hide-and-seek in the first place!"

Justin sat down next to him and was quiet for a few minutes. Then he stood up to walk around. "I think it's hiding. I think it's a game, and we need to figure out how to find it."

Spencer decided not to respond. He continued to hold his head. He needed to think.

"This room is so cool!" Justin exclaimed from across the room. "Great places to hide."

Spencer stared blankly at the floor.

"Let's keep playing hide-and-seek, and maybe the door will show up."

Spencer lifted his head and glared at his brother. "Seriously? You think we should play right now? You think that will get us back home?"

"I don't know. But we're stuck here, so let's play."

"I don't feel like games right now, Justin. This is serious. I need to figure out how to get us out of here."

"Come on, Spencer. You didn't take your turn yet. Please? Just one game?" Justin continued to beg. Spencer thought about it. He didn't know what else to do. He figured he could play one more time, and then he'd search the room again.

"Okay, but just for a few minutes."

Justin smiled. "Your turn to hide!"

Spencer groaned. He stood up and looked around the room. Justin was already counting. Spencer spotted a shiny cube across the room that looked about his height. He ran over to it but didn't see a door. He looked around and saw that none of the cubes had doors. But there was a square opening, like a window. He crawled through and sat down close to the opening so he could get some light and more air. He looked around the inside of the cube,

51

but there wasn't much to see except the walls around him.

He heard Justin call out that he was finished counting. He was glad because it was getting stuffy in the cube. He wondered how long they had been gone. He thought about Lori. Did she know they were gone? Was she looking for them? She must be panicking. Had she called their mom?

He heard Justin's voice and pushed himself away from the window. As he did, he felt a small object under his hand. He picked it up and saw that it was a little square wooden piece. It looked like a game piece from his mom's Scrabble set. He held it up near the window and could see the letter "B" engraved in the wood. He put it in his pocket and pushed back into the corner as he heard his brother approaching.

Just then, it got darker in the cube. Spencer looked over, expecting to see Justin blocking the opening. Instead, he saw that the opening was gone. Spencer started to panic.

"Help! Help! Justin, help me!" Spencer pounded on the side of the cube, trying to break the wall down. "I'm trapped! I can't get out!" He continued screaming. He hoped Justin could hear him. His heart was beating fast, and he struggled to breathe. "Help!" It was getting hotter. He felt like he was suffocating. He tried to stand and push on the ceiling. He needed to get out of there. He knew he was going to die if he didn't.

Spencer sat down and started to kick with his feet. He was hot and sweaty and could barely breathe. Then the walls started closing in on him. *Why doesn't Justin hear me?* he thought. He kicked until he no longer could move. Then all became quiet.

CHAPTER 8

"Spencer? Hey, wake up!"

Spencer felt his body shaking. He opened his eyes to see Justin's face above his. *Was I sleeping?* He struggled to focus. He felt groggy. He closed his eyes to think. *Yes, I must have been sleeping. What a crazy dream I had. I'll have to tell Justin about it when I'm ready to wake up.* He smiled, relieved to be out of that nightmare. It had seemed so real.

"Are you okay? Wake up," Justin said, shaking him.

"Go away! Let me sleep," Spencer growled at him.

"No, you need more air," Justin said. "We need to get out of this cube."

Cube? Then it hit him that he wasn't at home in his bed. He remembered being trapped in the cube as the walls were closing in. Panicked, he tried to sit up. His head was spinning. He looked around. Behind Justin, he could see that the opening was back. He crawled over to it. His arms and legs felt weak as he pulled himself through the opening. He could feel Justin pushing him from the other side. He fell onto the floor outside the shiny cube and laid there, looking up at the odd, high square ceiling. His head was pounding. Justin crawled out and sat by him.

"Are you okay?" Justin asked.

Spencer could hear the concern in his voice. "What happened?"

"I heard you pounding on the side. And then you were quiet. Could you hear me shouting back at you?"

Spencer shook his head no.

"I'm sorry. It took me a while to figure out how to get to you."

Spencer lay on the floor and thought about what had happened. He realized that he could have died if it weren't for Justin. "The window disappeared. I was trapped. How'd you get to me?"

"The opening was hiding. I could see the outline of it, but it was solid. I figured I had to find it." Justin pointed to the window on the side of the cube.

"Hiding?" Spencer asked in disbelief. "It disappeared and nearly suffocated me!" He lay there clearing his head. "So how did you get to me?"

"I tried knocking through it. Nothing worked. I figured I had to find a way to make the window reappear," Justin explained. "I remembered seeing the square pieces hanging on the walls. I thought maybe I needed to find the one that matched the shiny material and the size of the outline. Once I found the right square and placed it over the spot, it opened up. That's when I saw you lying in there."

Spencer rubbed his temples. His head hurt, and he couldn't follow Justin's story. But he was grateful for his brother's quick thinking. Justin had saved him.

"The walls were closing in on me," Spencer said. "They were going to crush me."

Justin looked at him strangely. Finally, Spencer sat up. The little square wooden piece that he had found in the cube fell out of his pocket. Justin picked it up and looked at it.

"Looks like a piece from Mom's Scrabble set. But this has a number on it."

Spencer saw that the side Justin was looking at had the number "1" on it. "Flip it over," Spencer said.

Justin turned it over. He scrunched his face up in thought. "Is the 'B' letter worth one point? Is that why there's a '1' on the other side?"

"I don't know. I've played a few times but never paid attention to the points. But I think the 'B' is worth more than that."

"I think I saw other pieces like this when I was looking for you," Justin said, looking around. "We should find all of them and see if it's a clue. Maybe it'll tell us how to get out of here."

Spencer couldn't believe that Justin thought the piece was part of a clue. But he had been right about the clue on the marble. And Justin had saved him – he somehow had figured out how to get to him inside the cube. Spencer thought he'd better be nice and go along with the idea.

"Okay, let's look. But I'm not getting inside another cube," he said as Justin helped him stand up.

"I'll look inside them, and you look around the outside. If the opening hides on me, don't forget how to find the square on the wall that matches."

Spencer nodded. They started looking for pieces. After they finished looking throughout the room, they returned to the square table. Justin sat down on a square chair as they placed the wooden pieces on the table. There were fifteen pieces.

"Why do you think these game pieces are here, but there isn't a Scrabble board?" Justin asked, looking around. "I mean, why aren't there any other games in this room?"

"Don't know," Spencer responded without looking up. He hadn't noticed that. He was busy turning the pieces to the letter side.

"What does it say? Is it a clue?" Justin asked excitedly.

"This makes no sense," Spencer mumbled after he had lined up all the letters. He noticed that one tile was blank on one side but had the number "7" on the other side. He knew for sure that the blanks in his mom's Scrabble game could be used for any letter but weren't worth any points. "Look at this," he said, holding up a tile. "This 'T' tile has a '3' on the back. There are three more tiles with a 'T,' and they have a '4,' '8,' and '12' on the other side. So, the numbers can't be the points for the letter."

His voice trailed off as he put the tiles in alphabetical order. "BEEEEGHORRTTTT," he said, trying to sound it out. He didn't know what to do with the blank, so he put it at the end. Then he started moving the letters around as Justin watched. "I'm trying to make words out of these letters," Spencer said. He knew Justin wouldn't be much help since he couldn't read very well. Spencer tried for a while and finally gave up and sat down on the square stump next to Justin. It was useless. They were stuck.

CHAPTER 9

Justin stood up and started turning the wooden pieces over to the number side.

"What are you doing?" Spencer protested.

"Maybe the game has something to do with the numbers," Justin said as he turned all the pieces over and put them in order from lowest to highest. The numbers went from 1 to 15. Justin studied the numbers for a minute.

Then he got excited and started turning them over again, but this time, in the order of the numbers on the back. When he was finished, Spencer looked at the words that were formed: "BETTER TOGETHER." Spencer saw that the space tile wasn't meant to be a letter — it was meant to separate the two words.

"Justin, you did it! I think you figured out the message!" Spencer smiled for the first time in a while. Justin beamed at the compliment.

Spencer stood and studied the message. "Better together." He noticed that "together" was in the clue for the second time that day — first on the marble, and now in the Scrabble pieces. But he wasn't sure what to do with it. There wasn't a door to open together. Spencer glanced up. The door was still missing. He studied the message. He realized that he kept thinking *he* had to get them out of there. He had thought it was all up to him. But in reality, Justin was helping . . . a lot. He saved Spencer. He had solved the clue. It was better when they worked together.

"Better together. Better together." He repeated the words, trying to figure out what to do next.

Justin stood up on the square stump and started saying it with him, waving his arms, just for fun. Then he looked at the wall. "Spencer — the door!"

Spencer spun around and saw that the square door was back on the wall. They left the pieces on the table and ran to the door. Justin placed his left hand on the square doorknob. He looked up at Spencer. Without saying a word, Spencer placed his hand next to his brother's. They turned the square knob to the right at the same time. The door opened for them. Spencer grabbed his brother's arm and pulled him through the door, afraid that it might disappear again. As soon as they were through it, the door closed.

"What just happened? The door disappeared and then reappeared?" Spencer stared at the square door. "How did that happen?" He was relieved to be back in the circular room but couldn't understand it. The door was there. Then it was gone. Then it was there again. He had felt around the wall after it had disappeared, and it was like a door had never been there.

"We figured out the clue," Justin said proudly. "I told you it was playing hide-and-seek with us."

Spencer looked at him. He wanted to tell Justin how crazy that sounded, but the whole afternoon had been crazy. "Maybe you're right," he said. He could tell from Justin's crooked grin that his little brother liked that answer.

"Let's pick another door," Justin said, looking around.

"No! We have to get back home. We need to see if we can get the hallway door to open. We have to get back to the slide." Spencer pulled his brother along with him to the giant black door. They both reached out and touched the metal handle together.

"It worked!" Justin said as the door

swung open a few feet. He stepped through the opening.

Spencer started to follow and then stopped. He looked back at the circular room of doors and the glowing blue marble in the center. He looked up at the four brightly glowing full moons on the ceiling as he stepped through the doorway. The large door closed gently behind him. He breathed a sigh of relief. He was actually happy to be back in the creepy hallway. Now they just had to figure out how to get back up the slide.

Justin ran ahead of Spencer to the slide. Spencer followed, glancing over at the strange walls. Justin bounced several times on the rubber mat in front of the slide. Then he tried to run back up the slide. He only got to the second turn before sliding back down. He tried several more times.

"It's too slippery!" Justin said as he slid back down.

"Let me try," Spencer said. He got a running start but slipped and landed flat on the slide. He tried several more times. He saw Justin removing his shoes and did the same. Still, neither of them could get past the second turn. Finally, they stopped.

"There's got to be a way back up. We have to figure it out. I must have missed something. We can't be stuck down here forever!" Spencer stood up and started looking around. Justin grabbed his shoes and sat on the edge of the slide to put them back on. Spencer walked behind the slide. It was dark, and he couldn't see much of anything. Then he heard a "whoosh" sound and a surprised shout. The shouting grew louder and then seemed to disappear. Spencer ran around to the front of the slide.

"What's wrong? What happened?" Spencer called. "Justin?" He looked around in utter shock. "Justin!" he screamed. Spencer felt his legs shaking as he struggled to stand. Justin was gone! *How did this happen, again?* He saw Justin's left shoe in front of the slide. "Justin, where are you?" he screamed. Spencer looked around but didn't see him anywhere. He knew he was there a second ago, sitting on the slide. He picked up Justin's shoe that was on the floor and sat down on the edge of the slide to think. *Where could he have gone?* He looked over to the wall. *Was it possible? Was there a creature in the wall, and did it take Justin?*

Suddenly, Spencer felt his hair stand up and a pull on his shirt. Something was tugging on him. He yelled out. *What is happening?* He heard a *whooshing* sound as he started to move. It felt like a giant vacuum was pulling him up like he was a little crumb. He was sliding *up* the slide! He flew around the turns as he held tightly onto his brother's shoe. He had gone backward on a ride before, but never backward up a slide!

A few seconds later, he slowed down. He was at the top of the slide. Spencer felt something push him off, and he rolled under the couch. He was back in his living room. While he was happy to be back, he knew he couldn't leave Justin behind. He had to go back! He felt around the floor and the back wall, but both were solid. He didn't know how to go through it. He needed help.

CHAPTER
10

Spencer lifted the couch skirt and crawled out. He was shocked to see Justin sitting on the living room floor, waiting for him.

"We made it back!" Justin exclaimed. He grabbed Spencer's outreached arm to pull him out from under the couch.

"I am so happy to see you! I didn't know where you went," Spencer said.

"I went *up* the slide! That was so awesome. I want to do that again!"

Spencer stared at his brother. His shirt was dirty and his hair, as usual, was a mess. But he looked as happy as he could be. He handed Justin his other shoe. Spencer realized this was the third time today that he was happy to see his little brother. He took a deep breath to calm down. "I thought you were lost down there again." He sat in silence for a minute. "We slid *up* the slide," Spencer finally said, shaking his head in disbelief. "We tried to climb it a hundred times. We sat on the edge and slid up. And it pushed us back under this couch." Spencer stared at the big cream-colored couch and thought. *How did we fall through? And how did we get back?*

"Wait here. I'm going to get a flashlight. I want to see what's under this couch," Spencer said, running upstairs to his room to get his flashlight. He ran back down to the living room two stairs at a time. He saw Justin still trying to tie his shoes. It always took him a long time to get his laces tied.

Spencer got down on his stomach and stuck his head under the couch skirt. Justin lay down next to him and stuck his head under as well. Spencer aimed the flashlight on the floor. Besides seeing disturbed dust, he didn't see anything unusual. He flashed it on the back wall. Everything looked normal. Spencer pushed himself under and crawled to the wall. He flashed the light on it and felt around. It was just a cold wall. He turned the light to look at the bottom of the couch but didn't see anything strange there either.

Spencer crawled back out and stood up. He looked at the old, oversized couch. "I don't get it. How did this happen?" He couldn't make sense of anything that happened that afternoon.

"It's magic!" Justin said. His eyes were big. "I think the couch is magic!"

Spencer sat thinking for a while. "I don't think we should tell anyone about this. I mean, not yet." He looked at Justin. He knew Justin talked too much. *Could he keep a secret?*

"But it was so amazing!" Justin said.

"Yes, but I don't think anyone will believe us. I'm not sure I believe what just happened. We need to keep this between us for now. Our secret. Can you do that?"

"Oh, I keep secrets all the time," Justin said, nodding. "I don't tell Mom half the things you do to me."

Spencer groaned. He needed to make sure Justin understood that he was serious. "Look, I know Mom and Dad won't believe us. But even if they did, they probably wouldn't let us go near the couch. Or maybe they'd get rid of it."

"No, they can't get rid of it. I want to go again!"

"Then keep it our secret for now," Spencer said. "I want to figure out how it happened. There's something strange about this couch."

"I told you, it's magic!"

"Let's see what we can find out about it from Dad. I'll ask him at dinner tonight."

"When is dinner?" Justin asked. "I'm starving!"

"I have no idea what time it is," Spencer said. He looked out the window and saw the workers still busy on the lot next door. It was still light out. Then he remembered Lori. Spencer swung his head around to look toward the family room. He had forgotten all about her. "Oh no! Lori is going to be so mad at us. I bet she's been looking everywhere!" Spencer hoped she hadn't called his parents or the police. He didn't know how they were going to explain being gone so long. "We're going to be in so much trouble!"

Spencer ran into the family room, with Justin at his heels. Spencer could feel his heart pounding as he tried to think of a story to tell her. He stopped as he got to her chair. He could see her feet on the footstool. He softly called her name. His voice cracked, and he clasped his hands together to keep from shaking. His mind was blank. He couldn't think of what to tell her!

"Lori?" he called again. She didn't respond. He walked around and glanced at her face, expecting her to be upset. Instead, he saw her eyes were closed and her mouth slightly open. She was softly snoring. She was asleep! Spencer couldn't believe their luck. He looked over at Justin and smiled. Then he looked at the TV and was shocked to see that her program was still on. That didn't make any sense. He looked back toward the kitchen at the clock on the wall. He couldn't believe what he saw.

"Justin," Spencer whispered. "According to the clock, we weren't gone very long." Spencer looked at the second clock on the microwave. It was the same time as the clock on the wall. It felt like they had been gone for several hours. But between the clocks and the TV program, he saw that they had only been gone for minutes, not hours. He let out a sigh of relief as he fell onto the couch next to Lori's chair. Her show was still on, and she was fast asleep. It was possible that she didn't even know they were gone.

Spencer heard Justin giggle. He looked up and saw Justin tickling Lori's face with his finger. He watched as Lori swatted at her face, and he tried not to laugh out loud. His brother was such a rascal. Finally, Lori scratched her face and opened her eyes. She straightened her glasses and looked at the boys.

"Oh!" she exclaimed. "Are you finished playing hide-and-seek?" Spencer knew she didn't want them to think that she had fallen asleep. She looked at the TV and then sat up in her chair.

"I'm starving!" Justin told her.

"Well okay then. Let's go get a snack." She slowly climbed out of the chair as Justin ran to the kitchen.

At dinner that evening, Spencer asked his dad a ton of questions about the couch. He learned that his dad had bought the couch at an antique store in the mountains from a sales lady who thought the couch was 150 to 200 years old. She said it had belonged to an old woman who lived in the mountains her entire life. The sales lady believed that the old woman's grandfather had built the couch. She said that the family had been in the mountains as long as people around there could remember. After the old woman died, her son sold some of her things to the antique store.

Then his dad went into detail about how massive and well-built it was. He went on and on about how they didn't build furniture like that anymore. He wondered what it looked like before someone had recovered it with the cream-colored fabric. The boys didn't get much useful information after that.

CHAPTER
11

Later that night, when the boys were in their rooms and ready for bed, Justin opened Spencer's bedroom door. Usually, Spencer didn't allow him to come into his room. Justin stood in the doorway.

"Today was so much fun! I want to go back tomorrow. I want to ride that slide again." Justin was talking loudly, as usual.

Spencer shushed him and waved him in. "Shut the door!" He didn't want their parents to hear. Justin walked over and stood by Spencer's bed.

"Can we go again tomorrow?" Justin asked.

"No! I don't think we should ever go back. Don't you realize how lucky we were to get home today? What if we had gotten stuck there?"

"But we didn't," Justin responded. "We figured it out and got back. Besides, there were so many doors. I want to see what's behind *all* of them."

"We don't know anything about that strange place. Or what's behind those doors." Spencer saw that Justin didn't like his answer. "Look, I could have died in there today. It's just too dangerous." Spencer shuddered at the thought of nearly being suffocated in the cube.

"But you didn't! You're fine." Justin sat down on the bed. "Come on, Spencer. We have to go back. Imagine all the amazing adventures we can have!"

Spencer couldn't believe that Justin wanted to go back there. The afternoon had been so stressful. He was worried the entire time. He didn't know if they'd ever get home. Spencer had already decided they weren't going back. Justin would just have to accept it. He hoped he wouldn't try to go by himself.

"You know you can't go alone. You can't get through that big metal door without me." Spencer watched his brother, making sure he understood.

"I know. That's why I want you to go," Justin said, looking pleadingly at Spencer.

"No," Spencer said, shaking his head. "That's my final answer." Mindlessly, he reached his hand up to touch the round silver pendant that he wore on a black braided leather chain around his neck. His grandmother had it made for him for his tenth birthday. It was a special gift. She knew he loved space, so she had it made with a crescent moon and stars on one side and the infinity symbol on the other side. He loved the unique design and that he could wear the pendant either way. He knew that space was infinite, and he liked that infinity was bigger than any number. It was hard for him to imagine space and infinity. Spencer's stomach sank as he reached around his chest for the pendant. His necklace was gone!

"Justin, I'm missing the pendant that Grandma gave me!" he cried as he jumped off his bed. He began searching his room. "Have you seen it?"

"No," Justin said, scrunching up his face to think. "Did you take it off to take a shower?"

"No. I don't usually take it off." Spencer crawled around on the floor, looking for it. "And I know I had it on earlier today." He tended to touch it when he was anxious, and he had been very anxious that afternoon.

Justin ran into the bathroom to look for it.

"If I ever take it off, I put it on my nightstand," Spencer said, looking around.

After searching his bedroom and bathroom, he collapsed on his bed. "I must have lost it under the couch."

"I'll go look for it," Justin said, starting toward the door.

"No, I mean on our adventure. I would have seen it under the couch earlier when I was looking with the flashlight. I think I lost it in the square room," Spencer said, closing his eyes to remember. "I know I was touching the pendant when I was suffocating in the cube."

"We'll go back tomorrow and look for it," Justin said happily.

"Noooo!" Spencer groaned, putting his head in his hands. "I can't tell Grandma that I lost it. She'll be so disappointed with me," he said, remembering how happy she was when she gave it to him. He sighed heavily.

"I bet we'll find it if we go back. And this time, I promise I'll hold the door open," Justin said. He could see that Spencer wasn't convinced. "I promise!"

Spencer shook his head back and forth.

He never planned to return to that place. Now he knew he had to. He had to find his chain and pendant. Finally, he nodded. "Okay. We'll go back. But only one time — just to find my necklace."

"Yay!" Justin yelled, jumping around. "I can't wait to ride that slide again. And I get to pick the door."

"No Justin, we're just going to go back to the square room to get my necklace."

Justin frowned. "But I want to go on another adventure."

Spencer sighed. "Look, let's get there and find my pendant first. Then we can discuss it." He just wanted to get his pendant back.

Justin quickly agreed. He turned in circles around the room, happy to be able to go under the couch again.

"But remember your promise to me? You don't tell anyone about it. And you *only* go there with me. Promise?" He raised his pinky finger, and Justin shook it.

"I promise."

"Besides, it takes the two of us to open a door," Spencer reiterated.

"I know. We have to go TO ... GET ... HER."

CHAPTER
12

Once Justin had settled down, the boys talked for a long time about their adventure. Justin told Spencer how it felt when he was alone at the bottom of the slide, hoping that Spencer would hear his calls. They talked about riding on the slide, the circular room with all the doors, the starry ceiling with the four full moons, and the glowing marble.

Spencer studied his brother's face as he went back through how he found Spencer in the cube. As he retold the story, Spencer still couldn't believe that Justin had figured out how to find the square opening. He thought about how angry he had been at Justin earlier in the day. He had teased him a lot lately for being stupid because he couldn't read well. He had to admit that Justin showed a lot of creativity solving the clues to help them get back home. He had spotted the word on the marble. He had saved Spencer in the cube. Then he figured out how to solve the message on the Scrabble pieces.

"You know, Justin, you did a good job today. You solved the Scrabble message."

"Better together," Justin said, nodding.

"And I still don't know how you figured out how to get to me inside the cube."

"The opening was playing hide-and-seek, just like the door to the room," Justin said, looking happy that Spencer was saying nice things. Justin continued, "I'm glad you found me today! I would still be stuck down there if you hadn't." Spencer felt guilty. He had thought about going up to his room and not looking for Justin any longer. He couldn't imagine what would have happened to Justin if he had done that.

The boys sat in silence for a minute. Justin started yawning as his eyes grew heavy. Spencer shook Justin with his leg. "Get out of my room. Go sleep on your own bed."

Justin crawled off the bed, rubbing his eyes. Then he grinned. "I can't wait until tomorrow!"

Spencer watched his brother leave. Justin was wearing his dinosaur pajamas. He had showered, and his blond hair was neatly combed back. Spencer moved his book aside and turned off his light. He reached again for his pendant and then remembered it was lost. He didn't want to go back under the couch, but he had to find it. He couldn't tell his grandmother that he had lost her special gift.

He leaned back on his pillow and looked up at the new glow-in-the-dark moon and stars on his ceiling. He had helped his dad put them up a few days earlier. These were better than the ones he'd had at his old house. He knew he was ten now, but he still liked to see them at night before falling asleep. He thought about the domed ceiling in the circular room with all the bright stars and moons. It looked so real. He had never seen so many stars. He still didn't understand the four full moons. His bedroom ceiling had one moon. He also had formed the Big Dipper on his ceiling with seven big stars. He hadn't recognized any formations on the domed ceiling. He planned to look at his book on stars to learn more formations before they went under the couch again.

As he stared at his ceiling, he replayed the day over again in his head. He had mixed feelings about going back. The day had been stressful for him, but it also had been pretty incredible. He was excited to see the domed ceiling and blue marble again. He thought about what he saw while sitting on the marble. He didn't tell Justin about that. Seeing the boy who looked like him was so strange. And he could still recall the awful pain the boy felt in his heart without his brother. Spencer knew what it meant. He knew that he would be miserable without Justin. He hadn't been nice to him lately. He had been fighting with him a lot more than usual. It was because he was so mad about the move and leaving his friends. He was mad about being stuck with his brother all summer. But today's events showed how much he needed Justin. And they had fun . . . despite how stressful it was.

Spencer smiled. What had started as a rotten day ended up being amazing. The summer was starting to look a little brighter. Although he missed his friends and his old house, he had to admit that he was looking forward to the next day and going back under the couch . . . with Justin.

SUSAN LINTONSMITH went from climbing the corporate ladder to falling under the couch.

Susan grew up in Colorado, where she loves sports, the mountains, and spending time with her family and two dogs. She is the mother of two teenage boys and dreamed of writing books based on the stories she told them when they were young. With the support of her husband and sons, she took a break from her 30-year business career to follow her dream.

Her goal is that all kids, especially those who struggle with reading like her boys, will enjoy the adventures Spencer and Justin go on in the Under the Couch series.

Visit her website at underthecouchbooks.com.

Look for the next two books in the
Under the Couch series,
Rainbow and *Spiders*.

Made in the USA
Columbia, SC
12 November 2021

48828355R00062